L.A. NOIR

He saw the lights spread out below as the jumbo jet ascended over the Pacific, a glittering web brighter than the stars. The HOLLYWOOD sign was floodlit against the distant hills, an invitation and a warning.

ROBERT FERRIGNO
Dead Man's Dance (1995)

L.A. NOIR. A POST-CHANDLER PORTRAIT OF LOS ANGELES IN THE WORDS OF THE FICTIONAL PRIVATE EYES, COPS, SHAMUSES AND DETECTIVES WHO'VE PROWLED ITS MEAN STREETS.

EDITED BY STEVEN GILBAR
PHOTOGRAPHS BY PETER TREADWELL

Positive Press
Chico, California

ISBN   0-9671960-0-0

FOREWORD

I drove my usual shortcut through a residential section of tiny stucco bugalows. Raymond Chandler country --I imagined that behind every screen door sat a peroxide blonde in curlers and a frowsy negligee.

LINDSAY MARACOTTA
The Dead Hollywood Moms Society (1996)

Raymond Chandler set the tone. It was dark, it was sardonic, it was, well, noir. The writers gathered here are his literary sons and daughters. The detectives they have created in their novels, like Chandler's Phillip Marlowe, are usually outsiders looking at Los Angeles with a jaundiced eye. They probably give as good a perspective on the place as you can get in fiction. And often in the richly metaphoric, often comic, Chandler style. Sometimes it can be almost parodic; take this, for example, from Keith Laumer's homage to the master, *Deadfall* (1971):

The streets were almost empty at that hour. I drove over to Santa Monica, cruised aimlessly west past closed stores as bleak as a pauper's funeral, past all night cut-rate liquor stores as garish as a Chinese wedding, past used-car lots like elephant graveyards, as gay as a rainy day at the orphanage.

This is piling-on, but the quotes in this book, I think, you will find more restrained yet mostly inspired by Chandler and worthy of him. I am not a scholar of detective fiction and offer no analysis nor deconstruction of the genre; I am just a common reader of them, especially if they take place in L.A., of which, like many of you, I have a love-hate relationship. This is, I think, reflected in the quotes selected here: a bouquet of dark roses, accompanied by the dusky photographs of Peter Treadwell. An umbered homage to the city of angels.

The individual photographs do not illustrate the quote on the page opposite to them; rather they are intended to complement them. Or, perhaps, it is quotes which complement the photographs. In either case, they seem to work together.

Driving the Mustang out of LAX an hour later, Bosch rolled the windows down and bathed his face in the cool, dry air. The sound of the breeze through the grove of eucalyptus trees at the airport gateway was always there like a welcome home. Somehow, he always found it reassuring when he came back from his trips. It was one of the things he loved about the city and he was glad it always greeted him.

MICHAEL CONNELLY
The Last Coyote (1995)

The weather had changed; it was now bona fide "June Gloom"; the dense marine layer no longer rolled in and out, but sat permanently, day and night, on silent haunches all along the beach, brightening only for several hours in the afternoon. Some people find this romantic in a Dickensian hansom-cab-and-gaslight way, but to me it just feels claustrophobic, as if I'm trapped in a humongous pill jar sealed up with thick cotton wool.

LINDSAY MARACOTTA
The Dead Hollywood Moms Society (1996)

Southern California reaches out to its visitors. The warmth of the sun, the sight of the San Gabriel Mountains, dry winds from the desert, the bitter herbal smells of the brushwood flowers, the orange poppies in the bright-green landscape that has not yet suffered the cruel fate of summer--at this time of year all these things urge me to stay forever.

LEN DEIGHTON

Spy Hook (1988)

The vast city was just awakening as I sped eastward on the Santa Monica Freeway. . . . Between the freeway and the Hollywood hills the feathery light of early morning poured into the basin and it truly did seem, at that moment, to be the habitation of angels. The great palms lifted their shaggy heads like a race of ancient, benevolent animals. Along the broad boulevards that ran from downtown to the sea, skyscrapers rose abruptly as if by geologic accident but were dwarfed by the sheer enormity of the plain.

MICHAEL NAVA
Goldenboy (1988)

I almost had a feeling that I knew the place without having been there before. L.A. had always been that way with me. It was familiar, it belonged in my unconscious; it enthralled me, enticed with all the ambivalence of a dream. Good, bad, indifferent things happened here, but somehow you believed they worked out; and even if they didn't, you kept believing. This city makes you soft and soppy, turns you into mush. Like a star-struck girl with an autograph album, you run amok thinking there's an answer to be found here--all because you've spent too much of your life sitting in the dark. And the big screen begat a small screen, and the small screen begat you.

MURRAY SINCLAIR
Only in L.A. (1982)

It always seemed to me Los Angeles was about being somebody you weren't to begin with but maybe could be with a little work and a lucky break or two. People drifted here from all over the world to change who they were.

ROBERT M. EVERSZ
Shooting Elvis (1996)

By the time we got back to the building, the sun had dropped behind the skyscrapers to the west so that a purple sci-fi glow softened the stone exterior. There is a natural but theatrical order to things here in Los Angeles. The cinematographer's golden patina of afternoon. Then the pink or orange sunset made glorious by smog. Purple. Fade to black. In the parking lot where I'd left my car next to the movie theater, a film crew was beginning to set up a ring of tungsten lamps. Framing a shot. That happens here, the conversion of street corners to sets. A certain unreality of location, and uncertainty of time.

MERCEDES LAMBERT

Dogtown (1991)

Jack Liffey remembered looking out over L.A. in April, 1992 with a profound sense of unease as roving gangs torched department stores and Korean mini-malls, and pillars of dark smoke rose all around the horizon, like burnt offerings to malign gods. Back then he'd finally located the unease: his sense of a world that was steadily getting worse, and nobody gave a damn, nobody was putting anything but token effort into fixing things, as a sort of social entropy carried the whole country down into chaos. The poor suffered, the rulers turned their backs and the rich retreated into armed enclaves.

JOHN SHANNON
The Concrete River (1996)

In Los Angeles there are seven days out of the year that are so spectacular you feel lucky to be alive . . . and to own a convertible that is running again. . . . Today is one of those seven days. . . . Looking inland you can see snow-capped peaks sixty miles away; sailing west every discrete fold in the Santa Monica Mountains is visible, every window in the towers of Century City shines. The sky is filled with rare sign of white and charcoal clouds thick enough to cast rippling shadows across a sparkling metropolis newly born.

APRIL SMITH
North of Montana (1994)

La Ciudad de la Reina de Los Angeles--Jessie's ninth-grade Spanish teacher had taught them the full name: City of the Queen of Angels. The queen and her angels were long gone; they'd probably moved to some small town in Oregon where the air was clean and the streets were safe. That's what everybody else in L.A. whom Jessie talked to was doing lately.

ROCHELLE MAJER KRICH
Angel of Death (1994)

I sat on my porch listening to Bach's French Suite Number Six and watching the sun come up over the San Gabriels. Dawn could be beautiful in L.A., misty-gold the way it must have been a few hundred years ago when Father Serra first eased his fat Spanish ass down the Camino Real.

ROGER L. SIMON
The Big Fix (1973)

The city was golden, blinding, blasted by heavenly light. It was one of those days that made nipples rise and minds wander and bodies shiver with sensuality and inexplicable dread. The kind of day when the heat wrapped snugly around you but sent an ominous chill up your back at the same time, like the first sexual touch in a dark room from a beautiful stranger whose name you'd never know.

JOHN MORGAN WILSON
Simple Justice (1996)

It was July. Hot winds that felt like the devil's breath blew into Los Angeles from the desert, rattling through the shaggy eucalyptus trees like a dry cough.

JOHN MORGAN WILSON
Simple Justice (1996)

They call October in L.A. "the fire season." It's a euphemism. A bad October, and this was a very bad one, is a month of fearsome, random firefall. Black ashes flutter down from the sky, to paraphrase Dickens, like snowflakes gone into mourning for the death of the sun. Except that in L.A., we get the sun, too, drying the air and driving the winds, fierce Santa Ana winds that clear the smog and then fan the flames to spread dark streaks of smudge across the sky like finger marks on a wall. In October the pool cleaners of Beverly Hills work overtime, straining ashes from the surface of placid blue water.

TIMOTHY HALLINAN

Incinerator (1992)

We're on an amusement park ride called the Hollywood Freeway, ripped out of our gourds, flying through the turns, with the rest of the traffic to the rollicking k.d. lang's band on the country-western station. The music propels us along in the dazzling thrall of a necklace of diamond headlights and glittering, swaying clusters of ruby-red taillights, stretching forever before us. The rumbling trailer trucks are giant prehistoric ants that we speed by in the darkness, and the bright roadside signs call out, proclaiming their readiness to fill your needs. . . Best Western . . . Chevron . . . McDonald's . . . California Federal . . . Familiar symbols that tell you you're safe, they're out there, you're not lost, you're not alone . . . We're doing 75 synchronized to the dance of traffic, rolling in, rolling out, fast and sleek in the sable night . . . The Broadway . . . May Company . . . Denny's . . . Taco Bell . . . They're always with us, always there for you.

DAVID DEBIN
Nice Guys Finish Dead (1991)

The rain had started again, a thick, grey downpour that slowed homeward-bound traffic on Wilshire Boulevard to a fitful crawl and made drivers champ their jaws in unison as they cursed the idiot ahead. There was an opening in the curb lane and I slipped into it, turning right some two or three blocks past Doheny. Behind me a horn blasted out of pique or jealousy or both.

ROSS THOMAS
The Singapore Wink (1969)

On the drive home the air cloaking the freeway was raw with chemicals. You had to work to breathe it, and the harder you worked, the worse headache it gave you. Visibility was about fifty yards. On either side the neon-lit wilderness of junk-food stands and body-repair shops softly glowed and winked in the haze. I drove fast, changing lanes, trying to make time, hurrying out of habit, though I knew there was nothing waiting at home except a half-read novel, an open bottle of Scotch, and an unmade bed.

TIMOTHY HARRIS
Good Night and Good-Bye (1979)

At 5:55 she was at the mouth of the mighty Ten, underneath the sign that said: CHRISTOPHER COLUMBUS TRANSCONTINENTAL HIGHWAY. She waited for the light to change and finished her mascara. . . . At the green light, she orange-lined the TR and tore down the Ten going ninety with one eye in the rearview mirror and one hand touching and punching the stereo's buttons like braille and one-half a mind to drive on. Let's drive. Goddammit. Past Grand Avenue, past L.A. City, L.A. County, past the rest of it, flowing with the current of the Ten, a straight shot to Jacksonville, Florida.

DIANNE G. PUGH
Cold Call (1993)

The cops found Andrew Brown trying to limp away from the school. He was the definition of a loser in L.A.: A man without a car.

WALTER MOSLEY
A Little Yellow Dog (1996)

They were standing outside the restaurant under the canopy, night air swirling smells of jacaranda and garlic and exhaust around them. Sunset Boulevard was a time-exposure photo of taillights and frozen billboards advertising the latest beauty product and cop buddy-flick. Above the strip the Chateau Marmont frowned on the traffic and late-night antics, as Marianna thought, Isn't that were they found Belushi dead?

PHILIP REED
Bird Dog (1997)

I drove out Sunset to my office. The Strip was lighting up for business again. The stars looked down on its neon conflagration like hard bright knowing eyes. . . . The night-blooming girls and their escorts had begun to appear on the Strip. Gusts of music came from the doors that opened for them.

ROSS MACDONALD
"The Suicide" (1954)

"The famous Trocadero once stood right there," and the ride to the office became a tour of Sunset Strip, Harry pointing out mostly where places used to be. Schwab's drugstore, Ciro's, known for movie-star bar fights, now the Comedy Store. A restaurant that was once John Barrymore's guesthouse. The Garden of Allah, where movie stars used to shack up, now a bank and a parking lot. The Chateau Marmont was still there--look at it--home on and off to Jean Harlow, Greta Garbo, Howard Hughes, off into Old Hollywood. Then telling what it was like when hippies took over the Strip. Little broads in granny dresses, traffic bumper to bumper. "By the time you got from Doheny to here, you were stoned on the marijuana fumes."

ELMORE LEONARD
Get Shorty (1990)

The Sun Tree Gallery of Beverly Hills rested atop a jewelry store two blocks from Rodeo Drive amidst some of the world's most exclusive shopping. There were plenty of boutiques with Arabic or Italian names, and small plaques that said BY APPOINTMENT ONLY. The shoppers were rich, the cars were German, and the doormen were mostly young and handsome and looking to land a lead in an action-adventure series. You could smell the crime in the air.

ROBERT CRAIS
Stalking the Angel (1989)

They have murders in Beverly Hills about as often as rent parties. . . . In any other city . . . there was a murder there'd be lots of black and whites, ambulances, TV press vans, patrolmen yelling get outta there, keep moving. Beverly Hills called for maybe one detective, couple guys to cart off the· remains, so smooth as easily a pile of laundry, and a press agent to keep it out of the papers.

STAN CUTLER
The Face on the Cutting Room Floor (1991)

[It] was one of those quiet palm-lined avenues which had been laid out just before the twenties went into their final convulsion. The houses weren't huge and fantastic like some of the rococo palaces in the surrounding hills, but they had pretensions. Some were baronial pseudo-Tudor with faked half-timbered facades. Others were imitation Mizener Spanish, thick-walled and narrow-windowed like stucco fortresses built to resist imaginary Moors. The street was good, but a little disappointed looking, as though maybe the Moors had already been and gone.

ROSS MACDONALD
The Barbarous Coast (1956)

I packed an overnight bag and drove around awhile before deciding on the Bel-Air Hotel as a good place to recuperate. And hide. It was just minutes away, quiet and secluded behind high stucco walls and towering subtropical shrubbery. The ambience--pink exterior, forest green interiors, swaying coconut palms, and a pond in which flamingos floated--had always reminded me of the old mythical Hollywood--romance, sweet fantasy, and happy endings. All of which seemed in short supply.

JONATHAN KELLERMAN
Blood Test (1996)

Sighting cars over the steep cliffs bordering the highway was part of life for residents of the Mulholland corridor--it happened with regularity in all kinds of weather. Its precipices, shrouded in dense growth, were a favorite venue for murders, suicides, dumping bodies and stolen cars, and speed freaks losing it around the treacherous curves. Street gangs ran regular drag races along Mulholland on Saturday nights. Some won, some lost, and some took the long, long plunge.

KELLY LANGE
Trophy Wife (1995)

I had the top down and we could hear dogs barking from the deep shadows of the canyon and the desolate tinkle of music from the houses that clung to the hillsides like would-be suicides waiting to jump.

JOHN MORGAN WILSON
Revision of Justice (1997)

Hazen Drive [up in the hills north of Sunset off Coldwater Canyon] was narrow and quiet, the houses the usual jarring mix of new and old, gaudy and gaudier. Most were set back from the road behind walls with remote-controlled iron gates. None were small. None would fetch less than two million, no matter what the economy was doing. The entertainment business constantly generates new millionaires. And discards old ones. Zorch's was a fine example of the early mishigothic style of architecture, complete with turrets, stained glass windows, and ivy-covered walls.

DAVID HANDLER
The Boy Who Never Grew Up (1992)

Cruising Hollywood Boulevard, Wil took in the dazzle. The City of Dreams lived in the bright billboards, the few remaining deco facades, the glowing marquees. Real Hollywood, though, lived at street level--in the human pinballs who bounced around mumbling, in the hungry angry ones snarling for spare change, in the timid vacant ones who avoided eye contact. Bits of human flotsam, they streamed and eddied past leather shops, greasy spoons, curio dives, low-fi outlets, T-shirt emporiums--the new inheritors.

RICHARD BARRE
The Inheritors (1995)

I gestured at the city lights that smoldered like an endless, fiery grid below us. "You don't believe in the Hollywood Dream?"

"I did when I came here," he said, sighing. "But then I discovered that Hollywood was just another small town in America, with a cop, a judge, a fag, a whore, and little Timmy who got run over in the second grade. Those pretty lights are just gaudy neon sign on run-down movie theaters and liquor stores with dirty floors. Most of the people here will wind up dead, in jail, or barbecuing steaks in the backyards of middle-class tract homes in suburbia."

ARTHUR LYONS

Three With a Bullet (1984)

[She] lived in the Los Feliz area, not far from the Planetarium and Greek theater in Griffith Park, up high on the bulge of a short curlicue of a street that had a view toward downtown which romanced you with a crazy quilt of dazzling lights and dim stars, like a lovely aging lady given to theatrics, showing herself to best advantage by night. By day, you knew she'd have to hide behind a killer smog to punish anybody rude enough to scrutinize her blotchy sallow pallor.

MURRAY SINCLAIR
Goodybye L.A. (1988)

Guido lives in a rugged canyon behind the Hollywood Bowl, his small gem of a house surrounded by groves of eucalyptus and dusty pine. Though he is only ten minutes from the festering armpit of the city--his description-- once you turn off Highland Avenue and start up his winding road you are deep in wilderness. So, okay, maybe it's an illusion of wilderness and locals dump their bodies off the side of his road with scary regularity. Still, at night coyotes howl at the moon from the rise behind his house.

WENDY HORNSBY
Bad Intent (1994)

It seemed to Rina that Hollywood got uglier and dirtier with each passing year, that the gentrification that was always being touted was just a word in the dictionary. And now with the Metro rail . . . all the construction and soot and dust and microorganisms being thrown into the air. Not to mention the bizarre parade of human flesh. Hard to believe this place was still a major tourist spot. But there they were, all nationalities, wearing short-sleeved Hawaiian shirts even in the winter, toting cameras around their necks. And the local inhabitants. Unisexual sleaze with greasy hair, torn jeans, vests, and tattoos. What wasn't covered in ink was studded with pierces. They must never fly commercial airlines Rina thought, because they'd never make it through the metal detectors.

FAYE KELLERMAN

Serpent's Tooth (1997)

Hollywood, the physical Hollywood with it's low-rent lifestyle, is where you end up when everything else you ever planned on, or dreamed about, or hoped for in life didn't pan out. The air stinks of desperation, take a deep breath and see if you don't choke on the hopelessness

JOHN RIDLEY
Love is a Racket (1998)

The area around Western and the freeway had been hit hard by the riots. Buildings had charred gaps and empty lots between them like a landscape of rotting teeth. I was ambushed at a red light by a man with a Windex bottle and a squeegee. The knife tucked into his waistband convinced me that he deserved a dollar. A scrawny man in front of a sex shop shook his hand at his side as if he was rolling dice. Crack for sale.

KEVIN ALLMAN
Tight Shot (1995)

Second Street took me across the long-disused stretch of railroad or streetcar tracks, lined with buildings of old, grimy brick, four or five stories tall, with faded signs painted on them and plywood over their windows. Once they had been factories, or vegetable warehouses, or even hotels. They all had the same dismal Edward Hopper rectangularity, the blind sadness of buildings with no one in them, buildings that have given over to the tenancy of spiders and rats and warp and rot.

TIMOTHY HALLINAN
Incinerator (1992)

The sun dawned me on [the downtown] streets gaunt without people. The area seemed oddly vacant, a studio oddly empty. Windows seemed shuttered from perversity rather than need. The few shops that opened were scored with graffiti, abusive and delirious. L.A. clocked early didn't look a going concern. It looked raddled, sickening for something, yet feverishly determined to conquer. The walls of buildings are pockmarked, as if firing squads had lately been about their business. Vacant ground wore skeletalized cars lying lopsided with one cheek into the ground. I walked enough to be pervaded by the sense of Los Angeles, which is action deflected beyond control, omnipotence revealing its secret neuroses.

JONATHAN GASH
The Great California Game (1991)

Guidebooks misrepresent Los Angeles as a sun-kissed amalgam of beaches, palm trees and the movies. The literary establishment fatuously attempts to penetrate that exterior and serves up the L.A. basin as a melting pot of desperate kitsch, violent illusion and variegated religious lunacy. Both designations hold elements of truth based on convenience. It's easy to love the place at first glance and even easier to hate it when you get to sense the people who live there. But to know it, you have to come from the neighborhoods, the inner-city enclaves that the guidebooks never mention and artists dismiss in their haste to paint with broad, satiric strokes.

JAMES ELLROY
Silent Terror (1986)

The spires of iron and tinted glass were not far from the Rancho. The buildings seemed like the towers of an industrial magus whose secrets the commoners in the lowlands could barely comprehend, let alone attempt to master. The starkness of what those close, yet leagues distant, buildings cutting above the landscape represented to the residents wasn't lost on anyone. The populace of the Rancho didn't go to lunch over two-dollar fizzy water, wondering if they could catch the play at the Dorothy Chandler while trying to get the prospectus modemed to San Francisco.

GARY PHILLIPS
Bad Night is Falling (1998)

The house in south central Los Angeles was set on a cross street devoid of shade trees or any other pretensions to beauty. The tiny houses were packed closely together, erected by a builder who comforted himself with the sure knowledge that he would never have to live in any of them.

JOHN BALL
Then Came Violence (1980)

Silver Lake was the Los Angeles capital of schizophrenia. It was Caucasian and Hispanic, gay and straight, young and old. It was picturesque, and it was garish; quaint and charming here, plastic and phony there. It had outdoor cafes and 7-elevens; health food stores and porn shops; three-story Tudor houses that dated back to 1911, and two-story towers of glass and steel that weren't yet a year old. In short, Silver Lake was a multilingual, multicultural, architecturally diverse community that offered a little something for everybody. Including the dumb and dumber.

GAR ANTHONY HAYWOOD
When Last Seen Alive (1997)

Bone Street was local history. A crooked spine down the center of Watts' jazz heyday, it was four long and jagged blocks. West of Central Avenue and north of 103rd Street, Bone Street was broken and desolate to look at by day, with its two-story tenementlike apartment buildings and its mangy hotels. But by night Bones, as it was called, was a center for late-night blues, and whiskey so strong that it could grow hairs on the glass it was served in. When a man said he was going to get down to the bare Bones he meant he was going to lose himself in the music and the booze and the women down there.

WALTER MOSLEY

White Butterfly (1992)

The barrio of East Los Angeles is one of those abandoned places where few dreams are achieved and too many of those that are end in sudden death. A cosmic brown hole from which little escapes. . . Some dying minor planet, a meteor-devastated world on the far side of the City of the Pueblo of our Lady of the Queen of the Angels . . . A dying planet crowded with creatures who couldn't save it and didn't even really want to try. A different life form. Not the same as those who lived on the green and comfortable power planet so many light years away at the other end of the freeway.

MICHAEL COLLINS
Cassandra In Red (1992)

In this part of East Los Angeles, without the preamble of chain-link fences or front lawns, the street intruded with all its noise and violence directly into people's living rooms. The only greenery was the jagged anise plants that sprung stubbornly from the cracks in the sidewalk.

LUCHA CORPI
Eulogy for a Brown Angel (1992)

[He] passed rickety wood-frame houses in need of paint, where radios blared mariachi music through rusty window screens, and little brown Mexican kids swarmed in yards where no grass grew. He braked the Electra at Sunset for a red light. Across the broad curving stream of traffic lay the park with the little lake, the ducks in the rushes, the muggers in the bushes, the sunburned tourists rowing battered little skiffs and peering through Instamatics at the glass skyscrapers beyond the tops of palms.

JOSEPH HANSEN
Skinflick (1979)

The street around us was a midnight carnival. Derelicts, hypes, a broad assortment of the ambulatory insane, spilled out of MacArthur Park like leakage from Pandora's box, to panhandle or rage against internal demons, to look for another fix.

WENDY HORNSBY
Midnight Baby (1993)

To the east, the ghetto communities of Compton, South Gate, and Lynwood were rigidly subdivided in to gang turfs where some fifteen to twenty homicides marred the average weekend. Here, there were only endless drab buildings decorated with angular territorial declarations thrown up by the taggers with cans of black spray paint. Wait until future cryptographers resurrect those stone tablets. Even the passing city buses were defaced, mobile messengers bearing insults from one gang to the next.

SUE GRAFTON
"H" is for Homicide (1991)

They turned off Ventura Boulevard in Studio City, a community of mismatched architecture: Spanish, Cape Cod, Tudor, colonial, and postmodern homes jammed side by side. It had been named for the old Republic Studios, where many low-budget Westerns had been shot before the advent of television. Most of Studio City's newest residents were screenwriters, painters, artists, artisans, musicians and craftspeople of all kind, refugees from gradually but inevitably decaying neighborhoods such as Hollywood, who were now engaged in a battle of life-styles with the older homeowners.

DEAN KOONTZ
The Door to December (1985)

Marina Del Rey, where wealthy singles, stewardesses, and recent divorcees flocked looking for hard bodies, development deals, and tropical drinks. Once, Charlie thought about moving to Marina Del Rey just to get laid, but took one look at the prices and decided he was better off celibate in Reseda.

LEE GOLDBERG
My Gun Has Bullets (1995)

It was after three, and the briefly clear night air had fallen to a sudden calm. There was no wind. The revealed moon tossed a bridge toward me, across the ocean; it swayed and rippled silver, a lifeline in the ever-changing waves. I gunned the Porsche fast down Coast Highway, sweeping by the cheap motels, the murky cocktail lounges, the spanking new malls, the antique and guns-and-ammo stores. The smoke and twinkling lights of the Redondo Beach refinery seemed less a glowering image from a German Expressionist movie than a forest of pipes and soaring steel.

RICHARD RAYNER
Murder Book (1997)

Santa Monica, a notoriously softhearted town, had at first pitied and tolerated its homeless, even supplying them with shelter and hot meals. But the city was wearying of its burden and now hoped, maybe even prayed, that its permanent underclass would migrate elsewhere, ideally to some spot far, far way such as Wyoming or Alaska or even Palm Springs,.

ROSS THOMAS
Voodoo, Ltd. (1992)

The second-story view from the window was of another apartment house. In Santa Monica, a blocked ocean view was the sign of an affordable address.

GERALD PETIEVICH
The Quality of the Informant (1985)

The westside chapter of the Society for the Prevention of Cruelty to Animals was sandwiched between warehouses on a cul-de-sac in the industrial section of Santa Monica--a collection of storage buildings and body shops near the bus station. Shopping carts full of derelicts' worldly goods parked in doorways served as declarations of homesteading claims. Blanket rolls, layers of newspaper, and empty wine bottles spilled onto the sidewalk. Mace couldn't help but wonder about a civilization that sheltered and fed the stray animals and left the humans to face the elements alone. Of course, the hospitality extended to animals lasted only so long. No easy answer.

BARBARA SERANELLA
No Human Involved (1997)

When viewed at a distance, from the water's edge, Ocean Front Walk is colorful, quaint, and bustling. It's not until you get up close that you realize how tawdry it is and that the people, even the young ones in their scanty bathing suits, firm flesh well displayed, are all burn outs. Even the "straights," citizens who live elsewhere and lead perfectly respectably lives, come to Venice for a Sunday outing at the shore and take on a certain sleaziness.

LES ROBERTS
The Lemon Chicken Jones (1994)

In the cool darkness of the garage I found a random tape and slapped it into the cassette player. The Doors "L.A. Woman" drifted out of the speakers as the garage door opened, revealing the Pacific Coast Highway in Malibu. PCH as itís known to the nine million denizens of Los Angeles County. I revved the engine of my car, a black Lamborghini Diablo I had picked up used a few months earlier, trying to warm it to the point that I could feel safe attempting intercourse with noonday traffic.

TERRILL LANKFORD
Shooters (1997)

The sun was shining in Hollywood, but a thick fog had wrapped up the coast. It was no great loss. The best thing about Malibu is the name. Once you get past the name and all its associations of movie stars taking moonlit swims, it's just a bare, uninspired stretch of sand fronted by a lot of overpriced beach shacks, tract houses, and quickie condominiums. The beach is narrow and the water is cold and the flimsy houses are too closely packed together. Most of them aren't much more than stucco fruit crates on stilts with a view of the ocean which you can't see for the fog. The Pacific Coast Highway runs by everyone's front door so you've got the roar of traffic all day, not to mention hideous rush-hour congestion and sea gulls ruining the paint job on your Rolls.

TIMOTHY HARRIS
Good Night and Good-Bye (1979)

The Malibu Colony is an exclusive seaside pocket of an exclusive seaside community on the western rim of La-La Land. It's a stretch of sand where motion picture and television stars live in isolated grandeur, sharing lobster and champagne suppers and the dread suspicions that the mobs are gathering outside the gates.

ROBERT CAMPBELL
Alice in La-La Land (1987)

The Valley, you know, L.A. is surrounded by valleys, but there's only one Valley, and to everybody who lives on the other side of the hills from it, it's a standing joke. All the same, a couple of million people manage to get along out there, and nobody's forcing them to stay. They keep their spades and aztecs penned up in Pacoima and San Fernando, and they vote Reagan, and when the smog comes on strong and the heat they lock their doors, turn on the air conditioning and wait for the next santa anas to blow it away. Sure, it's not a s picturesque as it used to be but what is? I guess all I mean to say is that it gripes my ass when the smart money in Mansonland starts laughing at the Valley. They ought to open their eyes and look out their own picture window.

PETER ISRAEL

Hush Money (1974)

There wasn't a cloud in sight. Birds of paradise, orange trees and stubby pines lined the streets. Sprinklers pumped water onto the emerald lawns. Mexican gardeners trimmed ivy. In the distance was heard the persistent drone of a leaf blower. Such are the charms of Sherman Oaks.

MERCEDES LAMBERT

Dogtown (1991)

I got past downtown and slowly began to leave behind the car dealerships and chain restaurants and motels that ooze away from Los Angeles like an old stain.

JEN BANBURY
Like a Hole in the Head (1995)

[U]nlike other cities, one leaves Los Angeles by increments from the crowded central city, over the canyons, through thickets of suburbs, until the tracts of houses thin into the remotest outskirts and then there are hills and sky and the freeway narrows to a two-lane road lined by eucalyptus, and the L.A. radio stations fade in and out, and it becomes possible to hear birds and smell the sea.

MICHAEL NAVA
Goldenboy (1988)

Sources

Allman, Kevin. Tight Shot. New York: St. Martin's Press, 1995

Ball, John. Then Came Violence. New York: Doubleday, 1980

Banbury, Jen. Like a Hole in the Head. New York: Little, Brown and Co., 1998

Barre, Richard. The Inheritors. New York: Walker Publishing Co., 1995

Campbell, Robert, Alice in La-La Land. New York: Mysterious Press, 1987

Collins, Michael. Cassandra in Red. New York: Donald I. Fine, 1992

Connelly, Michael. The Last Coyote. New York: Little, Brown and Co., 1995

Corpi, Lucha. Epitaph for a Brown Angel. Houston: Arte Publico Press, 1992

Cosin, Elizabeth. Zen and the Art of Murder. New York: St. Martin's Press, 1998

Crais, Robert, Stalking the Angel. New York: Bantam Books, 1989

Cutler, Stan. The Face on the Cutting Room Floor. New York: Dutton, 1991

Debin, David. Nice Guys Finish Dead. New York: Turtle Bay Books, 1991

Deighton, Len. Spy Hook. New York: Alfred A. Knopf, 1988

Ellroy, James. Silent Terror. Los Angeles: Blood & Guts Press, 1986

Estleman, Loren D. "Gun Music," Raymond Chandler's Philip Marlowe. New York: Alfred A. Knopf, 1988

Eversz, Robert M. Shooting Elvis. New York: Grove Press, 1996

Ferrigno, Robert. Dead Man's Dance. New York: G. P. Putnam's Sons, 1995

Gash, Jonathan. The Great California Game. New York: St. Martin's Press, 1991.

Goldberg, Lee. My Gun Has Bullets. New York: St. Martin's Press, 1995

Grafton, Sue. "H" is for Homicide. New York: Henry Holt & Co., 1991

Hallinan, Timothy, Incinerator. New York: William Morrow Co., 1992

Handler, David. The Boy Who Never Grew Up. New York: Doubleday, 1992

Hansen, Joseph. Skinflick. New York: Henry Holt & Co., 1979

Harris, Timothy. Good Night and Good-Bye. New York: Delacorte Press, 1979

Haywood, Gar Anthony. When Last Seen Alive. New York: G. P. Putnam's Sons, 1997

Hornsby, Wendy. Bad Intent. New York: Dutton, 1994

_____. Midnight Baby. New York: Dutton, 1993

Israel, Peter. Hush Money. New York: Crowell, 1974

Kellerman, Faye. Serpent's Tooth. New York: William Morrow Co., 1997

Kellerman, Jonathan. Blood Test. New York: Atheneum , 1996

Koontz, Dean. The Door to December. New York: Bantam, 1985

Krich, Rochelle Majer. Angel of Death.New York: Mysterious Press, 1994

Lambert, Mercedes. Dogtown. New York: VikingPress, 1991

Lange, Kelly. Trophy Wife. New York: Simon & Schuster, 1995

Lankford, Terrill. Shooters. New York: Forge, 1997

Laumer, Keith. Deadfall. New York: Crime Club, 1971

Leonard, Elmore, Get Shorty. New York: Delacorte Press, 1990

Lyons, Arthur. Three With a Bullet. New York: Holt, Rinehart , 1984

Macdonald, Ross. The Barbarous Coast. New York: Alfred A. Knopf, 1956

_____."The Suicide," Lew Archer, Private Investigator. New York: Mysterious Press, 1977

Maracotta, Lindsay, The Dead Hollywood Moms Society. New York: William Morrow Co., 1996
Maxwell, Thomas. The Suspense is Killing Me. New York: Mysterious Press, 1990
Mosley, Walter. A Little Yellow Dog. New York: W. W. Norton & Co., 1996.
_____.White Butterfly. New York: W. W. Norton & Co., 1992.
Nava, Michael. Goldenboy.Boston: Alyson Publications, Inc., 1988
Parker, Robert B. Perchance to Dream. New York: G. P. Putnam's Sons, 1991
Petievich, Gerald. The Quality of the Informant. New York: Arbor House, 1985
Phillips, Gary. Dead Man's Shadow. New York: Berkeley Prime Crime,1995
Pugh, Dianne G. Cold Call. New York: Simon & Schuster, 1993
Rayner, Richard. Murder Book. Boston: Houghton, Mifflin Co., 1997
Reed, Philip. Bird Dog. New York: Pocket Books, 1997
Ridley, John. Love is a Racket. New York: Alfred A. Knoph, 1998
Roberts, Les. The Lemon Chicken Jones. New York: St. Martin's Press, 1994
Seranella, Barbara. No Human Involved. New York: St. Martin's Press, 1997
Shannon, John. The Concrete River. Salem, OR: John Brown Books. 1996
Simon, Roger L. The Big Fix. New York: Warner Books, 1973
Sinclair, Murray. Goodbye L.A. Berkeley, CA: Black Lizard Books, 1988
_____.Only In L.A. New York: A&W Publishers, 1982,
Smith, April. North of Montana. New York: Alfred A. Knopf, 1994
Thomas, Ross. The Singapore Wink. New York: William Morrow Co., 1969
_____.Voodoo, Ltd. New York: Mysterious Press, 1992
Wilson, John Morgan, Revision of Justice. New York: Doubleday, 1996
_____.Simple Justice. New York: Doubleday, 1996

LA is a modern man's feeble attempt at paradise, a mirage of four million people rising out of the desert. Some Paradise. More like paradise lost.

What else could be said about a place where inhabitants live in constant fears of water shortages, brush fires, race riots, earthquakes, and God knows what else. Talk about shaky ground.

And I love everything about it.

ELIZABETH M. COSIN
Zen and the Art of Murder (1998)

Steven Gilbar has lived in California since 1970. His other anthologies include *Natural State: A Literary Anthology of California Nature Writing* and *Reading in Bed: Personal Essays on the Glories of Reading.*

Peter Treadwell has been taking photographs of Los Angeles for over twenty years. He now lives in New Hampshire.